About the Author

I have forever been excited about anything feathered, particularly those of the duck, goose and swan variety. By the age of thirteen, I was lucky enough to start my own collection, breeding various species of these charismatic & cheeky birds. Eight years later after graduating from university my affection had grown even stronger. At which point, I was eager to share this passion through writing a combination of informative and story-based books to inspire the upcoming generation to fall in love with nature.

I hope you enjoy the first book in the *Down at the Duckpond* series.

Edward

Down at the Duckpond with Carlton the Canada Goose

www.olympiapublishers.com
OLYMPIA PAPERBACK EDITION

A CIP catalogue record for this title is
available from the British Library.

ISBN: 978-1-78830-823-6

This is a work of fiction.
Names, characters, places and incidents originate from the writer's
imagination. Any resemblance to actual persons, living or dead, is
purely coincidental.

First Published in 2020
Tallis House
2 Tallis Street
London
EC4Y 0AB
Printed in Great Britain

Edward Giles

Down at the Duckpond with Carlton the Canada Goose

Olympia Publishers
London

Hello! and welcome to the pond.
Home to a goose we are truly fond.

And why does such a goose live on the
pond you might ask?
Dressed in a bright orange jacket and
wearing a face mask.

There is slowly moving water
for the occasional swim,
And green grassy fields,
to satisfy the appetite for him.

Squinting through the fine pair of
lenses sat upon his head,
Carlton noticed a strange object
floating on the pond ahead.

He wondered whether to tell others
before getting any nearer,
But didn't like the idea of sharing
so the choice wasn't clearer.

Besides, it is unlikely the swans
would be willing to share,
And the other ducks and geese,
would simply be a nightmare!

Carlton began paddling to
where the object lay,
Excited this could truly
be his lucky day.

Up alongside, he gazed at what
was a large wooden box,
And for a better view, leapt onto
a pile of nearby rocks.

Patting the top with his
glossy black feet,
Hoping inside could be
something to eat.

All he heard was a low thud,
so next he thought to try with his beak.
Tap tap, but nothing more, and only a
small hole through which to peak.

Back into the water he splashed,
in search for clues elsewhere,
So Carlton upended himself,
pale white bottom aloft in the air.

And there, the words
'Jumbo Rolled Oats' he found,
Those creamy, crunchy, crumbly
plump seeds and round.

But how and where did this box of
deliciousness come from?
"It is time for an adventure to find the
answer!" thought Carlton.

And so, as soon as sunrise
came the following day,
Carlton left the pond,
heading down the pathway.

First, visiting a boat yard, encountering
a gull to ask for some advice,
"Hello Gull, I wonder can you help, in
finding some oats to be precise."

"I'm sorry, but there is no such thing
around here," the gull said,
"I just help myself to the fish caught by
the fishermen instead."

"OK, thank you for your
help Gull," replied Carlton,
And soon he left, to continue the
adventure just begun.

Following the path through
the great green wood,
Carlton noticed a hawk in
front of where he stood.

"Hello Hawk! Would you mind coming
down so the two of us can speak?"
And with a shriek, up jumped the hawk
from the middle of its sleep.

"This better be important," squawked
Hawk, "to interrupt my rest."
"Indeed," Carlton remarked, "I've just
started out on a noble quest –

To find the source of some
oats on the pond yesterday."
"No, silly goose! Little birds and
mice are a hawk's usual prey."

Carlton turned away for a moment,
with a look of despair,
But when he turned back,
the hawk was no longer there.

So, without delay, he started back on his
journey once again,
When suddenly, the clouds turned grey
and down poured the rain.

Carlton scurried for shelter
under a nearby hedge,
Where crouched two beady eyed
pheasants at the far edge.

"Hello pheasants, would you know, where
I can find the source of some oats?"
But the pheasants did not answer, too
busy gobbling wheat down their throats.

Then soon the sky cleared,
And the sun reappeared.

So, Carlton left and began
climbing the nearby hill,
Soon he came across what
looked like a flour mill.

Approaching the doorway when out
swooped an owl,
"Hello Owl, have you seen some oats
during your prowl?"

"Yes, I have indeed," the owl replied,
"Brought from the farm on the riverside."

"Why thank you ever so
much for your help Owl,
I've come far from the pond,
leaving my fellow waterfowl."

So, off Carlton dashed with
a skip and a hop,
And wended down the farm
track to his final stop.

Arriving at the farm gate
with great excite,
Carlton couldn't wait to take
took his first bite.

There in front were those creamy,
crunchy, crumbly plump seeds and round,
And with no one else around, Carlton
flopped back on top of the mound.

Did you Know?

The Canada goose is the largest wild goose in the world.
When flying they form a V-shape to conserve energy.
After finding a partner they will stay together for life.
And can live between 10-25 years of age.
Besides oats their diet consists mainly of green vegetation.

Made in the USA
Middletown, DE
02 July 2015